MATT CHRISTOPHER®

On the Court with...

Jennifer Capriati

Matt Christopher®

On the Court with...

Jennifer Capriati

Text by Glenn Stout

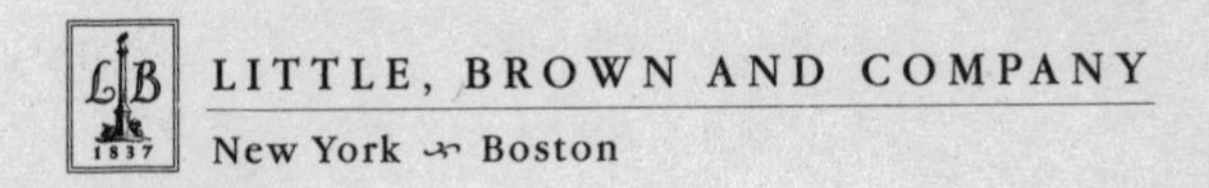

Little, Brown and Company

Time Warner Book Group
1271 Avenue of the Americas, New York, NY 10020
Visit our Web site at www.lb-kids.com

First Edition

Library of Congress Cataloging-in-Publication Data

Stout, Glenn.
On the court with . . . Jennifer Capriati / text by Glenn Stout.
p. cm.
Summary: Traces the life of the young woman who entered professional tennis at age thirteen and won a gold medal at the 1992 Olympics.
ISBN 0-316-16474-7
1. Capriati, Jennifer — Juvenile literature. 2. Tennis players — United States — Biography — Juvenile literature. [1. Capriati, Jennifer. 2. Tennis players. 3. Women — Biography.] I. Christopher, Matt. II. Title.

GV994.C36S86 2004
796.342'092 — dc21
[B] 2003046090

10 9 8 7 6 5 4 3 2 1

COM-MO

Printed in the United States of America

Contents

Chapter One: 1976–89 1
Born to Play

Chapter Two: 1990 15
Growing Up Fast

Chapter Three: 1990–91 28
A Lot to Learn

Chapter Four: 1991–92 36
Too Much, Too Soon?

Chapter Five: 1992–94 45
Unforced Errors

Chapter Six: 1994–96 54
Rehabilitation

Chapter Seven: 1996–98 62
Returning to Tennis

Chapter Eight: 1999 67
Comeback

Chapter Nine: 2000–01 74
Rising Up

Chapter Ten: 2001–02 82
More to Do

MATT CHRISTOPHER®

On the Court with...

Jennifer Capriati

Chapter One:
1976–89

Born to Play

The comeback is one of the most compelling stories in sports. Watching a team or an individual fight back from way behind or against long odds is exciting. So, too, is seeing a player compete again after suffering an injury.

But very few athletes in any sport have come back as successfully and dramatically as tennis star Jennifer Capriati. In 1990, at the age of thirteen, she became a professional tennis player. Within a year, she was ranked in the top ten in women's tennis. Most tennis observers expected that it would only be a matter of time before she became number one. She was one of the most famous athletes in the world, earning millions of dollars and appearing on the covers of dozens of magazines. Everyone loved her.

Although it seemed as if Jennifer had everything she needed, she wasn't prepared for her early success. She began to resent the way her entire existence revolved around tennis. Her progress as a tennis player stalled, and she stopped training. By 1995, she had given up tennis completely, and her personal life was a mess. At age eighteen, Jennifer was a has-been, best known as someone who used to play tennis.

Then, just when no one ever expected to hear from her again, Jennifer learned that tennis wasn't the cause of her problems. She discovered that she was responsible for her own happiness and that she still enjoyed playing tennis. She got her life together, resumed training, and within a very short time mounted one of the greatest comebacks in sports. Now, once again, Jennifer Capriati is one of the top-ranked tennis players in the world. This time around, she is determined to stay on top.

Jennifer Capriati began playing tennis almost before she was born. Her mother, Denise, was a flight attendant. On a trip to Italy in 1972, she met a dashing former soccer player named Stefano Capriati.

Stefano was handsome and athletic. Although he

was born poor, he had become very successful. After a brief career as a soccer goalie, he had become a stuntman in Spain, appearing in a number of movies. Denise and Stefano fell in love and soon got married.

For several years, they lived in both Spain and Long Island, New York. Stefano had taught himself to play tennis and was talented enough to work as a club pro in New York, teaching the game to others. Denise was one of his first students.

Even after she became pregnant with her first child, Denise continued to take tennis lessons. The day before Jennifer Capriati was born on March 29, 1976, Denise played tennis with Stefano. "He knew she would be a tennis player before she was even born," joked Jennifer's mother later.

Jennifer was a very precocious baby. She learned to swim before she could crawl and could swing on monkey bars before she could walk. Her father often took her to the tennis club when he gave lessons. She would chase loose tennis balls while he taught. Crawling around a tennis court was as normal for Jennifer as crawling around her own living room.

When she was three years old, Jennifer's father

gave her a racket and started teaching her how to play the game. At first, he concentrated on the basics, teaching her how to hold the racket and strike the ball.

Jennifer loved being with her father and playing tennis. Within a year, she was able to return balls shot toward her from a ball machine. Jennifer's little brother, Steven, chased after the loose balls just as Jennifer once had.

Her father was impressed by her ability and began to plan Jennifer's tennis career. To that end, the Capriatis moved from Long Island to Lauderhill, Florida, so Jennifer could play tennis all year long. Stefano began working in real estate.

Soon after moving to Florida, Jennifer's father decided that it was time for his daughter to take tennis lessons. He wanted her to learn from the best. A teacher named Jimmy Evert lived and worked in nearby Fort Lauderdale.

Jimmy Evert was a legend in tennis teaching. His daughter Chris was one of the best tennis players in the world. Jimmy had started teaching Chris the game when she was about Jennifer's age, and by the time Chris was sixteen, she was already a top-ranked women's player. Jennifer's father thought his daughter could be just as good as Chris Evert, perhaps even better.

He took Jennifer to see Jimmy Evert. Evert eyed Jennifer and asked her father how old she was. When Stefano said she was only four, Evert said "She's too young for me" and explained that he didn't work with students under the age of five.

But Jennifer's father was persistent. He begged Evert to watch her hit some balls before making a final decision. Evert agreed, and Stefano began hitting some balls to Jennifer.

Evert was stunned by what he saw. When the ball was to her left, Jennifer nimbly set her feet, held the racket with both hands, and fired a backhand shot to her father. When the ball was to her right, she held the racket with her right hand and deftly returned a forehand shot. On the rare occasion she missed a shot, she picked up the ball, threw it in the air, and served the ball straight back to her father.

She was the best four-year-old Evert had ever seen, much better than his own daughter had been at that age. In fact, Jennifer was already as good as some of the young students Evert was already training. Although she was small, she handled the racket well and obviously knew what she was doing, scurrying back and forth to get the best angle on the ball. Evert readily agreed to start giving Jennifer tennis lessons.

For the next five years, Jennifer spent several hours each week taking lessons from Jimmy Evert. She also played nearly every day with her father. When her brother, Steven, was old enough, he began to play tennis, too. Tennis became the most important thing in the Capriatis' life. Stefano and Denise arranged their schedules around their children's tennis lessons and worked extra hours to pay for them.

The object of the game of tennis is to hit the ball over the net so the opponent can't hit it back. But there is much more to the game than that. A player has to learn to read an opponent and to decide which shot will be most difficult to hit. She must learn to hit a variety of shots, such as forehands, backhands, lobs, and serves, and determine in an instant whether to return the ball hard or soft. She also must learn to put spin on the ball so that when it hits the ground, it will bounce in an unexpected way and hopefully fool an opponent.

These are known as the fundamentals of the game, and tennis players must learn to do them automatically, almost without thinking. That's why so many professional tennis players start so young, because the earlier a player learns the fundamentals, the sooner she can learn to play strategically.

Jennifer loved everything about tennis. She loved hanging out with her father and getting extra attention because of her ability. She didn't think there was anything abnormal about spending so much time playing tennis. It was her favorite thing to do.

As she grew older, she began to follow professional tennis, particularly the career of Chris Evert. Jennifer looked up to her. Not only was Evert a great tennis player, she was also beautiful, rich, and very nice. Jennifer even got to play tennis with her a few times, and Evert gave her a special gold bracelet for Christmas one year. Jimmy Evert told his daughter that Jennifer was the most talented young player he had ever coached. Jennifer began to dream about becoming a professional tennis player just like Chris Evert.

By age ten, Jennifer was running out of competition

near their home in Lauderhill. As Jimmy Evert later recalled, "She was beating every player in town." And that included the adults.

Her parents decided to relocate so Jennifer could continue to grow as a tennis player. They moved to Wesley Chapel, Florida, near the Saddlebrook Tennis Center.

The Center was a big school for tennis operated by a famous coach, Harry Hopman. Although Jimmy Evert had been a good coach, Jennifer was almost at the age when she could begin to compete in junior competitions. At Saddlebrook, she would learn to apply her skills in match situations.

Junior tournaments are for children under the age of eighteen and organized according to age groups. But from the very start, Jennifer rarely played against kids her own age. She was so good that she often had to play kids four or five years older to find some competition. The tournaments were quite competitive. Most players and their parents took them very seriously.

At first, Jennifer played in tournaments in Florida. But once she started to win, her mother and father began entering her in tournaments that required her to travel all around the United States and sometimes even overseas.

Jennifer loved traveling and staying in hotels. Although she sometimes had to miss school, she was a good student, and her teachers gave her homework to take with her.

Soon she was competing in the top junior tournaments in the country. In 1987, she teamed with Lisa Raymond to win her first national tournament, the United States Tennis Association (USTA) 14-and-under doubles competition. The following year, in 1988, she started winning singles competitions in major tournaments, taking both the USTA National Hard Court and National Clay Court junior titles.

Tennis can be played on a variety of surfaces, such as grass, clay, and what is called hard court, an artificial surface. On each surface, the ball reacts differently. Many players have a tough time adjusting. Some play well on clay, only to flub easy shots when playing on grass. Jennifer, however, seemed comfortable playing on all kinds of surfaces. That was an indication of her skill and adaptability.

The USTA victories made Jennifer stand out. Everyone in tennis was curious about her and wondered if she would become the next big star in women's tennis. In December of 1988, she was invited to play in an eight-player exhibition in Philadelphia, Pennsylvania. Jennifer, who was twelve years old, was the only amateur player invited.

She was excited before the exhibition match against eighteen-year-old Susan Sloane. Sloane was ranked number 30 in the world. The match flew by in a blur. Jennifer lost 3–6, 3–6 but impressed everyone with her tenacity and skill. In the second set, trailing 2–5, she fought off five match points, which are the winning points of the match, before finally being defeated. She certainly hadn't played like a twelve-year-old.

Jennifer was rapidly running out of competition from girls her age. In fact, Stefano Capriati thought that her recent performance demonstrated that she was ready to turn professional.

There were many issues to consider. Although the Capriatis were relatively certain that Jennifer could hold her own against the world's best tennis players, it was unlikely she would win right away. Although everyone believed that Jennifer would continue to improve, even the best tennis players lose occasionally. Jennifer would have to adapt to losing, something she had rarely experienced before.

She would also have to change the way she lived her life. If she played professionally, she would have to travel a great deal. Although her parents would often travel with her, that wouldn't always be possible. She would have to leave her friends, and there wouldn't be anyone else her age on the professional tour to hang out with. Although she would have a tutor, she would have to learn to study and keep up with her schoolwork on her own.

The Capriatis also knew that some people would disagree with the choice for Jennifer to turn pro. Many tennis observers had recently questioned whether it was a good idea for young players to become professional. They cited the experiences of both Tracy Austin and Andrea Jaeger. Like Jennifer, both girls had been tennis prodigies. Each had turned professional at age thirteen, and each had initially been quite successful.

But then each girl had experienced trouble. Both had been bothered by chronic injuries that may have been caused by playing too much tennis while their bodies were still growing. And as they got older, they had difficulty staying motivated and eventually resented their decision to turn pro. Tennis observers felt that the girls had "burned out" prematurely. By age twenty, both had retired from competitive tennis.

As a result, the Women's International Tennis Association (WITA) banned girls from playing professionally until age fourteen. At age twelve, Jennifer really wasn't in a position to make such an important decision herself. She had been playing tennis her entire life and had been dreaming about playing professionally for years. She was eager to turn pro but wasn't mature enough to consider the consequences of such a decision.

But Jennifer's parents thought she was ready. She was a good student at school, and they believed that her good grades demonstrated that she was responsible enough and mature enough to play professionally. Jennifer's father decided to petition the WITA and asked them to make an exception for Jennifer. "They made the age rule because of the burnout of two players," he complained. "But they don't know Jennifer. She gets straight As in school, and she's very healthy. She just wants to improve her tennis." After her thirteenth birthday in March of 1989, he wanted her to turn pro. But a month earlier, the WITA had rejected his request. Jennifer would have to remain an amateur for another year.

She took full advantage of her final year as an amateur. She followed a busy schedule, focusing on the so-called junior Grand Slam tournaments, which attracted the best players in the world. In June, she traveled to Europe to compete in the junior French Open. She won the tournament, defeating a player ranked number 134 in the world to become the youngest champion in tournament history. A month later at Wimbledon she and Meredith McGrath won the junior doubles title and Capriati reached the junior singles quarterfinals. She followed up with a victory in the junior U.S. Open and ended the year ranked as the number one junior player in the country and second in the world.

There was very little left for her to prove in amateur tennis. Jennifer and her family began to make specific plans for her professional career. Months before her fourteenth birthday, she was featured on the cover of *World Tennis* magazine. The buzz in the tennis world was that Jennifer Capriati would be the sport's next big star.

The first important tournament after her fourteenth birthday would be the Italian Open, a very prestigious event. But the Capriatis wanted Jennifer to begin her professional career closer to home.

Stefano Capriati petitioned the WITA again, asking if Jennifer could turn professional the month of her fourteenth birthday, which would allow her to play in a tournament in Florida. The WITA agreed.

Jennifer was turning pro. Childhood was over.

Chapter Two:
1990

Growing Up Fast

In March of 1990, Jennifer Capriati became the new heroine of women's tennis in the United States. She had some big shoes to fill. After a long, successful career, Chris Evert had retired at the end of the 1989 season. She had been one of the most popular women's tennis players ever and was credited with making women's tennis a prominent sport in the United States.

When Evert retired, there wasn't another American player to take her place in women's tennis. Although Martina Navratilova would eventually become an American citizen, she was from Czechoslovakia. Teen sensation Monica Seles was Yugoslavian, Steffi Graf was German, and most of the other top players were from European countries as well. American fans wanted an American player to root for. And the sport of tennis wanted an American champion as well because American sponsors and television networks provided much of the money that fueled the game.

Almost overnight, Jennifer Capriati became the next big name in women's tennis. Like Chris Evert a generation before, Jennifer was bright and bubbly and attractive. But Evert had been eighteen years old when she turned professional. It wasn't really fair for Jennifer to be compared to Chris Evert when she was not yet fourteen.

As soon as the WITA ruled in Jennifer's favor, her life changed dramatically. From the very beginning, she was under a lot of pressure. A number of companies looked at her and saw a future champion. They were so confident that she would succeed, they already wanted to have her endorse their products.

Jennifer and her parents tried to take advantage of the opportunities they were being offered without losing sight of what was really important — her happiness. As soon as they made the decision to turn professional, they signed with an agent, Jimmy Evert's son, John. The Everts had a great deal of experience in the tennis world.

John Evert helped the Capriatis negotiate a deal

worth $3 million with Italian clothing company Diadora. A tennis racket company and several other companies signed Jennifer to similar deals. At age thirteen, she became an instant millionaire. Of course, she didn't get all the money herself. Her parents took care of it for her. Like many teenage girls, Jennifer received an allowance.

Though such deals seemed to indicate confidence in her abilities to succeed, the decision to turn pro was controversial. The companies expected something for their money, so Jennifer was under some pressure to start winning right away. Critics kept comparing her to Tracy Austin and Andrea Jaeger, and they questioned the motives of her family, particularly of her father. Stefano Capriati was very involved in his daughter's life and career, and some people believed he was taking advantage of her for financial reasons. He scoffed at those who questioned whether she was prepared to turn pro. "They [Austin and Jaeger] were completely different," he said. "Jennifer is just an American girl with a chance to be great."

"My dream," said her father in another interview, "is that she keeps growing with this game."

In the weeks before Jennifer's professional debut, the Capriatis tried to keep her life as normal as possible. Jennifer did her best to ignore all the hoopla. She concentrated on playing tennis and on doing her schoolwork at the Palmer Academy, where she was a straight-A student in the eighth grade. Each day, she attended school from 7:00 to 11:00 A.M., then spent several hours practicing tennis and working out.

Still, it was almost impossible for Jennifer to continue to live a normal life. All of a sudden, everyone wanted to speak with her or get her autograph or take her picture. The Capriatis tried to take control. They limited access to their daughter as much as possible, allowing the media to interview her only at press conferences and encouraging her to spend her free time with her friends. But it was difficult to keep everyone away.

Jennifer's challenge was to stay focused. The life of a professional tennis player, although financially rewarding, can be very hard. The tennis tour lasts from February to November, with a new tournament almost every week. Yet playing tennis is usually the easiest part of it. What takes a greater toll is the amount of time spent traveling around the world to reach the competitions.

After arriving in a city for a tournament, players check in to a hotel and then try to practice some before the tournament starts. It is difficult to get enough rest. Once the tournament starts, it isn't any easier. Players usually compete each day until they lose. If they do lose, they often leave for the next tournament right away. If they keep winning, they have to stay. It is almost impossible for players to know precisely how long they will remain at a tournament.

But they have other responsibilities beyond playing tennis. Tournament sponsors often want to meet the players, so the players have to attend parties and other events. Fans want to meet them, too, and players are often called upon to give clinics and make other appearances. Many adults have a hard time adapting to life as a professional. Jennifer wasn't even fourteen yet.

Jennifer Capriati made her professional debut in March of 1990 in a Women's Tennis Association (WTA) tournament at the Polo Club in Boca Raton,

Florida. The tennis world was eager to see how Capriati would do. Although the tournament was considered a minor one, the press covered it as if it were a Grand Slam event.

Mary Lou Daniels was Capriati's first opponent. Although Daniels was ranked number 110 in the world, she had once been number 15. At age twenty-seven, she had been a professional for more than ten years.

When Capriati walked out on the court to warm up before the match, she was stunned by what she saw. The stands were full, rare for a first-round match, and photographers and other media representatives surrounded the court. But she felt more comfortable when she looked up in the crowd and saw a group of her friends from school holding up signs that spelled out "G-O J-E-N-N-I-F-E-R."

Capriati soon demonstrated that despite the difference in her and Daniels's age and experience, she belonged on the court. She got off to a great start, overwhelming Daniels with a blistering array of shots to take a 3–0 lead. The crowd was roaring with delight.

But Daniels had been behind in tennis matches

before. She didn't panic. She simply concentrated on making sound returns.

Now it was Capriati's turn to stumble. All of a sudden, her shots started going astray. She made a number of unforced errors, returning the ball either out of bounds or back into the net. Daniels pulled ahead 6–5. It appeared as if Capriati was going to lose her first professional match. People in the crowd exchanged knowing looks with one another. Capriati was good, but she was too young to compete professionally, they thought.

But they didn't know Jennifer Capriati. Just when everything looks hopeless, she can still rise to the top.

Now Capriati began to show some patience, focusing on her returns and making sure she didn't hand the match to Daniels with more unforced errors. Capriati rallied, tying the set at 6–6, setting up a tiebreaker. The first player to score 7 points would win both the game and the set.

With her confidence restored, the tiebreaker wasn't even close. Capriati streaked to a 7–1 win to take the set 7–6.

There was no stopping her now. In the second set,

Capriati grew bolder with each shot, and Daniels was helpless to stop her. Playing aggressively, Capriati displayed the full range of her talent. Her backhand was already one of the best in tennis. Fans loved the way she charged the net and forced her opponent to react when she could have stayed back and waited for her opponent to make a mistake. Her style was exciting and reminded many of former champion Billie Jean King's.

Capriati destroyed Daniels in the second set 6–1 to win the match. Afterward, she acted just like any other thirteen-year-old girl, laughing nervously as the press peppered her with questions, saying, "I'm excited about my match, but I think the media's a little out of control." Then she added, "It's all fun." So far, it was.

In tournament play, each competitor keeps playing until he or she loses. Capriati's victory in the first round meant she'd play again the next day. She faced Claudia Porwik, who was ranked number 34 in the world, and after a hard-fought battle, Capriati won. The following day, she faced Nathalie Tauziat, who was ranked number 16. Capriati won again. Now she would go up against Helena Sukova.

Sukova was ranked number 10 in the world and was favored by many to win the tournament. She stood over six feet tall and was one of the most powerful players in women's tennis. No one expected Capriati to advance so far in the tournament and beat Sukova — but she did. Then in the next match, she beat number 19, Laura Gildemeister, 7–6, 7–6. Suddenly, Capriati found herself in the tournament final playing against Gabriela Sabatini, number 3 in the world.

It was a tough match, but Capriati held her own against one of the best players in the world. In the end, however, Sabatini was simply too strong and experienced for her and won the match 6–4, 7–5 to win the championship. Still, Sabatini admitted, "I had to play my very best tennis to beat her."

No one had expected Capriati to make it so far in her first professional tournament. People suddenly saw that she wasn't just a good player — she was great! Bud Collins, a famous tennis writer and sportscaster, called her "the best American player since Billie Jean King." And Jennifer was still a couple of weeks away from turning fourteen!

As impressed as people were by Capriati's talent,

they were even more impressed by her personality. It seemed as if she was really enjoying herself; she was always smiling and telling people how happy she was. Even though everyone was complimenting her playing, it didn't seem to be going to her head. "I'm just a kid," she said. "I have this talent. I don't know why everybody is going crazy over it."

Over the next few weeks, she made an even greater impression on the world of tennis. Soon after celebrating her fourteenth birthday, she defeated Helena Sukova again in her second tournament before losing in the fourth round. In her next event, she reached the finals to face Martina Navratilova.

Although she lost the match, her playing had been solid enough to earn Capriati a WTA ranking as the twenty-fifth-best women's tennis player in the world — the highest debut ranking ever. Chris Evert said, "I wouldn't be surprised if she ended up in the top ten this year." Both *Sports Illustrated* and *Newsweek* featured her on the cover.

In almost every tournament she played in, Capriati's ranking improved. Even when she entered the larger international tournaments, she continued to beat players who were ranked higher and were much more experienced. She reached the quarterfinals of the Italian Open in Rome before losing to Sabatini but picked up the doubles title with Monica Seles, another teenage tennis sensation.

Then Jennifer played her first Grand Slam event, the French Open. The Grand Slam tournaments are the four most important tennis tournaments in the world: the French Open, the Australian Open, Wimbledon, and the U.S. Open. These tournaments are not only the most lucrative but also the most prestigious. Top players design their whole season around the Grand Slam events.

Capriati stunned the other players. She didn't lose a set en route to the semifinals, becoming the youngest semifinalist in tournament history. Her opponents were impressed. One said, "She keeps going after every shot, and that's different from the other players. When I played hard, she played harder." Although she lost to Monica Seles in the semifinals, her ranking jumped all the way to number 17.

Her amazing play continued at Wimbledon, the

prestigious English competition that is considered the most important tournament in tennis. Tennis players dream of winning Wimbledon the way baseball players dream about winning the World Series or football players dream about the Super Bowl.

Capriati was seeded twelfth, meaning that tournament officials believed she was the twelfth-best player in the tournament. Never before had a fourteen-year-old player been seeded at Wimbledon. In fact, no fourteen-year-old had ever even won a match at Wimbledon.

But Capriati wasn't like any other fourteen-year-old. She proved she belonged by winning her first three matches, earning the right to play Steffi Graf on center court in the fourth round of the tournament. Although she lost to Graf 2–6, 4–6, she was impressive. Graf, who at age twenty-one was already one of the best players in the world, expected to win easily. But Capriati forced her to play hard, and some observers blamed Graf's loss in the next round on how strenuously she had had to fight off Capriati the previous day.

About the only thing Capriati had yet to do was win a tournament. But that would come soon.

A week after Wimbledon, she was entered in an exhibition tournament at Mount Cranmore in New Hampshire. After Wimbledon, her agent and parents wanted her to play in an event with much less pressure. They wanted to make sure Jennifer had fun.

She had more than that. She ran the table, beating the field, including Rosalyn Fairbank in the finals, to win her first tournament. But she knew she still had a long way to go. "I hope to become number one," she said during the tournament, "but it's going to take a lot. I think I'm definitely not at the top, like the top five. I'm a level below that. I've played all the top players, like Steffi and Gabriela Sabatini, and I haven't come close to beating them. But I know what it takes."

That was becoming clear to everyone. It appeared as if it would be just a matter of time before Jennifer Capriati was one of the best tennis players in the world.

Chapter Three:
1990-91
A Lot to Learn

Capriati's impressive performance continued in the second half of 1990. She picked up her first WTA title in Puerto Rico, becoming the fourth-youngest player ever to win a WTA title. The victory was important because it qualified her for the Virginia Slims Championship, a year-end tournament featuring only those players who had won WTA events during the 1990 season. She had been playing well, and some expected her to sneak into the finals and maybe even win the tournament.

But for the first time all year, Capriati played as if she were running out of energy. Although Steffi Graf was ill with the flu, she still managed to defeat Capriati in the first round of the tournament. When the match ended, Capriati looked exhausted. She was ready for some rest.

In many ways, her first year as a professional had been a success. In addition to the millions she had earned for endorsements, she had picked up another $300,000 in tournament winnings and, more important, gained valuable experience. At the beginning of the year, no one was quite sure of her potential. Now there seemed to be no limit to how good she could become. Many tennis observers expected her to follow a path similar to that of Monica Seles. As a fifteen-year-old in 1989, Seles had made her debut on the tour, playing well and climbing up in the rankings, just as Capriati had done. But in 1990, her second year, Seles broke through to win a number of tournaments, including her first Grand Slam event, the French Open.

Capriati seemed on the verge of a similar breakthrough. She was still growing and, at five foot seven and 135 pounds, becoming much stronger. She had gained a lot of confidence in her first year as a professional. Although she had yet to defeat any of the top five players, she was playing them tougher each time.

But some in the tennis world were already cautioning that Capriati's career was going too fast.

They questioned the large number of tournaments she had entered in 1990. Older players like Martina Navratilova, who were still playing championship tennis in their midthirties, believed that one of the reasons she was still able to perform well was that she hadn't overdone it when she was younger. Capriati practiced for hours almost every day and then spent time lifting weights and working out.

Influential tennis writer Bud Collins had already criticized Jennifer's father for pushing her too hard. In response, Stefano Capriati reportedly told him, "You don't know if she's going to burn out. I don't know. Only God knows, but I tell you this, if she does we'll have more money than I ever imagined." Jennifer's earnings were supporting her entire family. Many people thought it was wrong for a fourteen-year-old to have that much responsibility.

At the same time, Jennifer was entering adolescence, which can be a difficult time. She was turning into a young woman, her body was changing, and she was beginning to become more independent. Like many teens, she would eventually want to exert more control over her own life. But for now, she simply did what her father and her agent told her to do.

And in the brief off-season, which lasted only a little more than two months, they told her to keep practicing and working out. Although she tried to spend as much time as possible with her old friends, she'd drifted away from many of them, and it was difficult to feel as close to them as she once had. In February of 1991, Capriati returned to competitive tennis.

Although she had played only a part-time schedule in 1990, in 1991 she went on the tour almost full time, seeing a tutor to keep up with her schoolwork and sending in her assignments by fax. She got off to a slow start, but by midsummer it appeared as if she were about to break through and take her place alongside Monica Seles, Steffi Graf, and Martina Navratilova as one of the elite players in women's tennis.

In July at Wimbledon, she faced defending champion Navratilova in the quarterfinals. In eleven previous meetings, Capriati hadn't come close to beating her.

But now Capriati was bigger, stronger, and smarter. She dominated Navratilova in the first set and then kept her focus in the second set despite a long rain delay. On the final point of the match, Navratilova returned the ball, then rushed the net, hoping to surprise Capriati, drive back a return for a winner, and mount a comeback.

Capriati was ready. As soon as she saw Navratilova charge toward the net, she changed her strategy. Instead of trying to hit a return down the side, she pulled up and flicked a backhand lob high and soft in the air, far over Navratilova's head.

As soon as Navratilova saw the ball going up, she stopped short. But it was too late for her to race back and try to return the shot. She watched helplessly as the ball drifted down. Her only chance would be if the ball were long and landed out-of-bounds.

But Capriati's touch had been perfect. The ball landed just inside the back line. Capriati had won!

The crowd roared, fully appreciating her shot. Navratilova was impressed, too. She couldn't help smiling a little bit herself. She even joined the crowd in their applause before shaking Capriati's hand.

Capriati was on a roll. She bulled her way into the semifinals versus Gabriela Sabatini to become the youngest player ever to reach that level at Wimbledon.

The two played a classic match. After losing the first set 4–6 and falling behind in the second set 4–5, Capriati dug in. Close to defeat, she gave Sabatini everything she had. Time and time again, she raced back and forth across the court, chasing down impossible shots and somehow finding a way to return them. She fought off match point four times before finally falling. Although she had lost, tennis fans were convinced that Capriati's performance at Wimbledon was evidence that she was on the brink of greatness and would soon fulfill her vast potential.

Over the next month, she played the best tennis of her life, first beating Monica Seles in the finals of the Mazda Classic, then winning the Player's Challenge tournament a week later. The back-to-back wins vaulted her to number 7 in the world rankings. With the U.S. Open just ahead, Capriati seemed poised to move up.

But just one day before the beginning of the U.S. Open, she played in a lucrative television exhibition against Gabriela Sabatini. Many tennis observers wondered if that was a wise move so close to the start of the Open. Yet at first it didn't seem to matter. When the Open began, Capriati roared through her early matches to the quarterfinals. There she faced Sabatini again — and this time she finally beat her, 6–3, 7–6. Capriati advanced to the semifinals to face the formidable Monica Seles.

Capriati was still playing great. Before the match versus Seles, fellow pro Mary Joe Fernandez spoke for many when she said, "The crowd will get behind her. Jennifer has beaten her [Seles], and she believes she can again. Her confidence is incredible right now. She's real hot."

Tennis fans were delighted with the matchup. The two teenage girls represented the future of women's tennis and seemed ready to embark on a rivalry as intense as that of Martina Navratilova and Chris Evert. Throughout the 1980s, these two stars had dominated women's tennis and engaged in a series of unforgettable matches. Capriati and Seles appeared destined to do the same in the 1990s.

The semifinals demonstrated just how well the

girls were matched. They split the first two sets. The winner of the third set would reach the finals.

From the start it was apparent that the last set would go down to the wire. Each player was at the top of her game, making impossible shots and impossible returns look routine. Capriati pulled ahead 5–4 and had an opportunity to serve for the match. But Seles couldn't be broken. She battled back to tie the set at 6–6, sending the match into a tiebreaker.

With the crowd roaring like they were at a boxing match, Capriati and Seles fought each other for one of the most intense tiebreakers in the history of women's tennis. In the end, Seles pulled it out 7–6 to advance to the finals.

Capriati was disappointed, but tennis fans were thrilled. One sportswriter called it "the single most extraordinary match ever between two players under the age of eighteen."

The extraordinary was beginning to seem pretty ordinary for Jennifer Capriati.

Chapter Four:
1991–92
Too Much, Too Soon?

After the Open, Capriati was exhausted. For the first time in her career, a loss had really bothered her. She felt as if she should have defeated Seles and gone on to capture her first major title. She believed she had let everyone down.

In the wake of her defeat, she took a break, returning home to Florida to spend some time being a fifteen-year-old girl rather than a fifteen-year-old tennis star — something that was becoming more and more important to her. She was maturing, and although she still loved playing tennis, there were other things she wanted to do. She was taking driving lessons and was looking forward to getting her driver's license when she turned sixteen. She liked listening to music, shopping, and going to concerts. She wanted to spend more time with her friends.

Over the past two years, she had been away from home so much that she was beginning to wonder if her old friends were still her friends at all.

She was also physically exhausted. She was still growing, which can be an exhausting experience in itself. Playing tennis on top of that left her feeling run-down. She just wanted to sleep and sleep.

Jennifer began to take it easy but still worked out with her coach and father. She knew that some of the people close to her thought she was easing up at the worst possible moment. After two months, she decided to start competing again.

But she didn't really want to. She felt as if she had to, and that made all the difference. Other players on the tennis tour noticed that she didn't seem to be very happy anymore, particularly when she had to be out in public. One tennis official commented that while she still appeared to enjoy playing tennis, she didn't seem to enjoy being a star.

Even though she reached the finals in her first tournament back, she lost to Monica Seles again. Then she pulled a muscle in her groin. She should have taken more time off to allow the injury to heal, but the Virginia Slims Championship was coming up. Although she could barely practice, she nevertheless competed in the tournament.

Somehow, she made it to the quarterfinals before losing to Gabriela Sabatini. Despite the two-month break and the groin injury, she still finished the season ranked number 6 in the world, her highest ranking ever. She had earned more than $500,000 playing tennis and almost another $5 million in endorsements. A magazine reported that she was the twenty-sixth-wealthiest athlete in the world!

But instead of taking the rest of the year off, she had agreed to play a series of exhibitions against Martina Navratilova. She played the exhibitions, but she didn't play very well, and Navratilova beat her easily. Many observers noted that Capriati wasn't playing with her usual enthusiasm.

In January, she traveled to Australia for the Australian Open and the start of the 1992 season. She lost to Sabatini in the quarterfinals. After the defeat, Capriati broke down in tears in her hotel. She desperately wanted to win the Grand Slam event, if for no other reason than to just get it out of the way.

Depressed, she then lost in the very first round of a tournament in Tokyo. She wasn't playing as if she wanted to be on the court. Exhausted both physically and mentally, Capriati simply wanted to go home. Her parents and agent tried to convince her to continue on, but she dug in her heels, and a big fight erupted. In the end, she was allowed to return home.

In many ways, what was happening between Jennifer and her family was absolutely normal. At some point during adolescence, most teenagers and their parents clash, usually because the parents still treat the teenager as a child while the teenager believes he or she is an adult. It often takes some time for the parents to recognize that the child is growing up, and it also takes time for the child to realize that the parents are just trying to do their best.

Jennifer Capriati's relationship with her parents was complicated by her tennis career. She was financially supporting her entire family. And in turn, they were doing all they could to help her career. But so far, her father and agent had made most of the decisions about her career. They had decided where and when she was going to play and what public appearances she would make. In her first year or two as a pro, that hadn't been a problem for her. But as she grew older, she believed that she had the right to start making some of those decisions on her own. She didn't always trust her father or agent to make the best choices for her anymore. Sometimes, she thought they wanted her to do things just so she could earn more money. She felt that she already had enough money and didn't need to do so much.

She argued with her mother and father over almost everything, from the way she wanted to dress to the music she listened to and the friends she wanted to hang out with. It didn't help their relationship when a magazine wrote a big story about her that claimed she had burned out just like Jaeger and Austin and that she was going to quit tennis. The magazine used some unflattering pictures of Capriati that embarrassed her. She later asked a reporter, "Why does everybody care?" She just wanted to be left alone.

Jennifer and her parents finally reached an uneasy truce. She would be allowed to make some of the decisions about her career. Her father, in particular, promised to withdraw and give her some more space. Because he had always made most of the decisions in her career, now he told a reporter, "She needs me as a father, not as a coach."

When Jennifer returned to competition in March of 1992, people immediately noticed that she had changed. She hadn't been working out very hard and had gained ten or fifteen pounds, making her look chunky. She had painted her fingernails black and let her hair grow long. Off the court, the girl who had usually dressed in preppy clothes now wore tie-dyed T-shirts and jeans.

Her attitude had changed dramatically, too. The press suddenly found her much less cooperative than before. She gave only one- or two-word answers to most of their questions and made it clear that she preferred not to be bothered at all. As a result, many of the stories written about her were critical, making her even less willing to cooperate. One reporter described her as "lost in a fog of adolescent alienation."

Her game, too, had undergone a change. She was no longer a consistent player. In big matches, against opponents like Monica Seles, she seemed to play well and to be trying very hard. But in matches against lesser rivals she should have defeated easily, her play appeared sloppy and halfhearted.

Her coach, Pavel Slozil, tried to encourage her to practice and work out more — in essence, to return her focus to the game. In May, they had a fight that resulted in Capriati firing him. This move hurt her reputation even more in the world of tennis. To many, it seemed as if her career was beginning to slip away. She didn't play well at the Italian Open, and at a press conference a writer asked her, "Do you think you lost because you are overweight?" Capriati collapsed in tears.

That's what made her performance at the 1992 Summer Olympics in Barcelona all the more surprising. Entering the Olympics, she hadn't won a tournament in nearly a year. Few people expected her to win a medal. Even a bronze medal for third place wasn't likely.

Just before the Olympics started, she hired a new coach, Manolo Santana. She enjoyed his workouts and started to regain some confidence. She arrived in Barcelona eager for the games to begin.

Capriati thoroughly enjoyed the Olympic experience. Olympic athletes all live together in the Olympic Village, where they have an opportunity to meet and get to know one another. There are so many athletes from so many countries that no one really stands out. For the first time in a long time, Capriati was not a star — and she loved it, particularly talking to athletes who had no idea who she was. She spent much of her free time in the Village cafeteria. "You just look for an open seat and sit down, and right away it's great," she later told a reporter. "You start a conversation with 'What country are you from? What sport?' "

When she took to the court at the Olympics, she was excited to be playing competitive tennis again, and it showed in her play. She swept through the early rounds to face Arantxa Sanchez-Vicario in the semifinals. Sanchez-Vicario, a native of Spain, had the crowd behind her the entire match.

But Capriati was so focused she barely noticed, not even when King Juan Carlos and Queen Sofia of Spain took seats at courtside in the middle of the match. "I didn't even know who they were," admitted Capriati later. She upset Sanchez-Vicario to earn the right to play in the finals against Steffi Graf. Even if she lost to Graf, she would still win a silver medal. But Capriati wanted gold.

Despite how well she had been playing, most people gave her no chance to beat Graf. Capriati had never beaten her before, and Graf was playing well. And at first, it seemed those people were right. Capriati lost the first set 3–6 but didn't get discouraged. "It actually gave me confidence," she said later. "It put a little more pressure on her." As the underdog, Capriati had nothing to lose.

She fought back to win the second set 6–3, then took a 5–4 lead in the third set. With the match and the gold medal on the line, it was her turn to serve. She and Graf battled for the game, but Capriati kept the upper hand. On match point, she blasted an ace past Graf to win the gold.

Capriati was thrilled when she took the podium and received her gold medal as the U.S. national anthem played. "It was unbelievable," she said later.

In a very different way, the next few years would also prove to be unbelievable for Jennifer Capriati.

Chapter Five:
1992–94
Unforced Errors

After her win at the Olympics, Jennifer Capriati's play sparkled over the next few months. It appeared as if she had put the problems of the past year behind her. She performed well in August and entered the U.S. Open as one of the favorites. After winning a gold medal, a Grand Slam championship seemed inevitable.

But once again, a Grand Slam event slammed Capriati. She lost in the third round, then stumbled through the remainder of the season. Although she finished the year ranked number 7, apart from her gold medal most of the season had been a disappointment.

Off the court, her life wasn't much better. She had turned sixteen and acquired her driver's license, which gave her some independence. But she still clashed with her parents, agent, and coaches over the course her career should take. As a high school student, she was suddenly expected to do a larger amount of schoolwork. Between keeping up with her studies and playing tennis, Jennifer felt as if she had no time to herself. In October, she was featured on the cover of *Tennis* magazine, her head buried in her hands, under the headline "Teen Turmoil."

At the beginning of the 1993 season, she was able to get by on her talent, winning her first tournament. In addition to the fact that she wasn't in very good shape, she was exhausted, and soon it began to show. She was hounded by all sorts of injuries and ailments, from pulled muscles to viruses to a sore elbow.

Emotionally, she wasn't much healthier. She was uncertain of how she really felt about professional tennis. Yet when she was unable to compete or she failed on the court, she felt terrible about herself and got depressed. And when she was depressed, it was even more difficult to train and play tennis.

Her experience at the U.S. Open was particularly painful. After opening her first match with a 6–1 win in the first set, she was upset by Leila Meskhi, who was ranked number 37 in the world. For a player like Capriati to lose in the first round was shocking to the fans and embarrassing for her.

After her defeat, she raced off the court in tears. She spent the next week in bed and later admitted that she had thought of killing herself. From her perspective, tennis was only bringing her pain. Although she had millions of dollars, she didn't have what she needed most — faith and belief in herself. Like Jaeger and Austin, Jennifer Capriati appeared to be burned out.

She withdrew from the Virginia Slims Championship in November and went into hiding. Rumors swirled around the tennis world that she was quitting tennis or quitting school or had run away from home. All the critics who had questioned the wisdom of her father's decision to have her turn professional at age thirteen looked like geniuses.

The Women's Tennis Council (WTC) decided to take action. They wanted to make sure that other young tennis players didn't turn professional too soon and encounter the same problems she had. One of Capriati's friends described her life on the tour by saying, "She was surrounded by agents, manufacturers, promoters — all people who were asking something of her. She couldn't share a lot, and I think it was isolating and lonely." The WTC didn't want any more teenage tennis stars to go through the same kind of experience. They announced that they would form a committee of experts to take a close look at the age eligibility rules for professional tennis.

But it was too late for Jennifer Capriati. The damage was done. As she explained later, "I always expected to be on top, and when I didn't win, to me that meant I was a loser. The way I felt about myself had to do with how I played, and if I played terrible I'd say, yes, I can handle it, but really I couldn't. I felt like no one liked me as a person. I felt like my parents and everybody else thought tennis was the way to make it in life. They thought it was good, but I thought no one knew or wanted to know the person who was behind my tennis life."

Yet without tennis, Jennifer didn't know who she was either. Finding out would be a painful and sometimes dangerous experience.

In December, she was shopping at a mall with some friends. They were looking at some rings in a kiosk at the mall. When they left the kiosk, a security guard approached Jennifer. She had walked away with a ring without paying for it.

Jennifer tried to explain that she had done so by accident, but the guard didn't believe her, and she was cited for shoplifting and arrested. Because she was a minor, the incident shouldn't have been reported, but somebody leaked the story to the press, and it was soon trumpeted all over the world that Jennifer Capriati was a shoplifter.

She was terribly embarrassed and ashamed. As someone who had made millions of dollars, she had no reason to take a $35 ring. She had made a terrible mistake, and her self-esteem and self-image had taken another blow.

Although Jennifer never admitted to taking the ring on purpose, many of the people who knew her interpreted the incident as a cry for help. It was as if she had almost wanted to get caught so people would understand how unhappy she was.

Over the Christmas holidays, she decided she didn't want to play tennis in 1994. She wanted to finish her senior year of high school and live a normal life without tennis and without other people telling her what to do. As one observer later noted, "She just got really tired of tennis. Not just indifferent — she came to despise it."

Her parents reluctantly agreed with her decision. "She's testing everybody," said her father. "She wants to see how they react to her if she doesn't play tennis."

Capriati stopped playing tennis entirely and didn't even bother to work out. After school, she spent her time running around, going to clubs, and staying up late. As soon as she turned eighteen, she quit high school and moved out of her parents' home and into an apartment with some friends. For the first time in her life, Capriati was on her own and able to do what she wanted when she wanted and with whom she wanted. But like many other young people who live on their own for the first time, Capriati wasn't really ready to live without any rules or restrictions.

Capriati didn't want to have anything to do with anyone she knew from the world of tennis. Her old friends rarely heard from her. She thought that most people had only paid attention to her because of her tennis stardom. Now she was determined to make new friends.

She met kids who knew nothing about tennis. Some didn't even know she had ever played tennis and was rich and famous. In a very short period of time, Capriati had an entirely new set of friends.

While some of them were genuine friends who shared Capriati's interests away from tennis, others weren't so sincere. They liked her because she drove a fancy sports car and had lots of money. When they went out with Capriati, she usually paid for everything.

Even though Capriati wasn't playing tennis, the press was still interested in her activities. Some gossip newspapers were reporting that she had become fat and had turned into a punk rocker with purple hair. Although she had experimented with dyeing her hair different colors and had gained weight, she wasn't quite as out of control as some of the newspaper accounts made it sound. But in May of 1994, that all changed.

One Friday evening, Capriati went to a party with some friends. Almost everyone was smoking marijuana and drinking, including Capriati. When the party ended, Capriati and her friends didn't want to stop. Capriati rented a motel room for everyone, and the extended party continued for the next two days. Friends called friends, and over the course of forty-eight hours dozens of people came by the room, some of whom Capriati didn't even know. The party was out of control — and Jennifer was, too. Whenever anybody needed anything, she would just hand over her bank card and the keys to her car.

Not surprisingly, most of the people attending the party proved to be fair-weather friends. When the police finally arrived to investigate the goings-on, Capriati was alone in the room.

The police searched her room and found marijuana in her bag. Capriati started crying. She was embarrassed and knew that she would end up in the newspapers again. "I don't want this attention," she pleaded to the police. "Let me call my lawyer." While they were still questioning her, an acquaintance and his girlfriend returned with Capriati's car. Police searched the couple and found crack cocaine and heroin. Capriati was arrested for possession of marijuana, and her friends were arrested on other drug charges.

Capriati was taken to the police station. She was fingerprinted and had to pose for a mug shot. Although she was released shortly after her attorney arrived to post bail, the mug shot photograph was released to the media.

Capriati's fans were stunned when they saw the picture. They hardly recognized the girl with the stringy hair and the nose ring. She didn't look anything like the athletic, enthusiastic teenage tennis star they were used to seeing.

That wasn't Jennifer Capriati anymore.

Chapter Six:
1994–96
Rehabilitation

In the weeks after her arrest, it was reported that Capriati had spent a brief period of time in a drug rehabilitation facility earlier in the spring. Two days after her arrest, she did so again, entering the Addiction Treatment Center of Mount Sinai Medical Center in Miami Beach.

All sorts of wild stories about her began to surface. Some of her new acquaintances cashed in on their "friendship" and sold their stories to magazines and television programs. They claimed that she was using all sorts of drugs and had been for more than a year.

But other friends told a different story. Although they didn't deny that Jennifer had been drinking alcohol and smoking marijuana the weekend of her arrest, they told reporters she was just "an eighteen-year-old girl living a normal life" who had gotten a little bit out of control. Capriati had even told them that the happiest moments of her life had been playing tennis, but that the pressure to become number one was too stressful.

The truth was probably somewhere in between, and Capriati has never spoken in detail publicly about her arrest or her stints in rehab. But those who knew her best blamed tennis for creating the situation.

One former coach said that the people around Capriati when she was on tour "looked at her only as a player. It was her identity. . . . Everyone wanted to take credit when things were going well, but when she had problems, people scattered." The former coach claimed that when Capriati first turned pro "she was the easiest, happiest kid I've ever known. After being on the tour for three years, I could see a change."

Former star Andrea Jaeger may have said it best. "I think a lot of this stems from not being able to do what she really wanted while she was young," she said. "In one sense, maybe this is the best thing that ever happened to her. Maybe this is the wake-up call."

Capriati stayed in the rehab clinic for twenty-three days. Patients in such centers are closely monitored so they don't continue to use drugs. They usually have to go to bed and wake up when they are told and participate in counseling sessions to discover why they have chosen to take drugs. Although the pressure she had faced as a professional athlete had certainly played a role in her problems, it was also important for Capriati to take responsibility for her own life. After all, no one had forced her to start taking drugs. But her hospital stay was just the beginning of her treatment.

After Jennifer checked out of the facility, her lawyer reached an agreement with the state attorney's office to settle her case. The state would drop the charges against her when she agreed to continue to receive treatment in a drug counseling program.

Now she had to rebuild her life and decide what role, if any, tennis would take in it. All her endorsements had been canceled after her arrest, and because she hadn't played for so long, she wasn't even ranked anymore. No one knew if she'd ever play tennis again. Fortunately, she didn't need to play

AP/Wide World Photos

The stress of losing overwhelms the sixteen-year-old Capriati after a defeat at the 1992 French Open.

AP/Wide World Photos

Olympic competitor Capriati wins the silver medal round by defeating her opponent 6–3, 3–6, 6–1.

AP/Wide World Photos

Gold medalist Capriati sheds tears on the podium during the United States national anthem in 1992.

AP/Wide World Photos

Capriati is despondent after losing a match in the 1996 U.S. Open; her defeat fueled doubts that she was really ready to stage a comeback.

AP/Wide World Photos

A few months after losing in the U.S. Open, Capriati celebrates after unseating the number one seeded player, Monica Seles, in the semifinals of the 1996 Ameritech Cup.

AP/Wide World Photos

Capriati raises a fist in victory after a match in the 1999 Australian Open.

AP/Wide World Photos

Capriati smashes a return back at Serena Williams in the quarterfinals of Wimbledon in 2001. Capriati won the match 6–7, 4–7, 7–5, 6–3 to advance to the semifinals.

AP/Wide World Photos

Capriati poses with her parents, Stefano and Denise, after her second consecutive Australian Open victory in 2002.

AP/Wide World Photos

Determination, speed, and skill combine in Capriati and boost her to victory in a match during the 2002 U.S. Open.

AP/Wide World Photos

Muscular and determined, Capriati gives it her all!

Jennifer Capriati's WTA Career Stats

Year	Singles			Doubles			
	Wins	Losses	W-L%	Wins	Losses	W-L%	Money Earned
1990	42	11	79%	6	7	46%	$283,597
1991	42	12	78%	16	8	67%	$535,617
1992	35	11	76%	5	4	56%	$315,501
1993	29	11	73%	2	2	50%	$357,108
1994	0	1	0%	0	0	0%	$4,575
1995	0	0	0%	0	0	0%	0
1996	16	11	59%	0	0	0%	$112,378
1997	10	12	45%	2	2	50%	$79,852
1998	17	14	55%	0	3	0%	$66,573
1999	27	14	66%	3	2	60%	$243,937
2000	36	19	65%	15	11	58%	$488,861
2001	56	14	80%	13	12	52%	$2,268,624
2002	48	16	75%	4	4	50%	$2,217,939
Fed Cup	10	3	77%	1	1	50%	n/a
Grand Slam	114	33	78%	22	21	51%	n/a
Main Draw	348	143	71%	66	54	55%	n/a
Total	358	146	71%	66	55	55%	$6,974,562

Jennifer Capriati's Career Highlights

1989:

Youngest player to win the French Open junior title
Won the U.S. Open junior title (singles and doubles); Wimbledon junior title (doubles)

1990:

Turned pro on March 5
Won first pro title at the Puerto Rico Open
Youngest player to 1) be ranked in the top ten, 2) be a semifinalist in the French Open, 3) win a match at Wimbledon, and 4) be seeded in Grand Slam history

1991:
Youngest semifinalist at Wimbledon (beating Martina Navratilova) and the U.S. Open

1992:
Gold medalist at the Barcelona Olympics

1993:
Dropped out of tennis after the U.S. Open

1994:
Returned for a short while, then left the tour again

1996:
Finalist at tournament in Chicago
Quarterfinalist in Essen, Germany

1999:
Won eight consecutive titles, her best performance in six years

2000:
Semifinalist at the Australian Open

2001:
Won the Australian Open
Won the French Open
Semifinalist at Wimbledon
Semifinalist at the U.S. Open

2002:
Won the Australian Open—fighting off four match points to win, a first in WTA history
Semifinalist at the French Open
Won the ESPY award for Best Comeback Athlete
Finalist at the Canadian Open
Semifinalist at the WTA Championships

tennis in order to support herself. She still had millions of dollars in the bank.

Tennis wasn't the most important thing in her life anymore. Learning how to like herself was.

She also had to repair her relationship with her parents. It was a painful and difficult time for the whole family. Stefano and Denise didn't trust her anymore. Jennifer still resented the way she had been pushed to turn professional at such a young age. Still, she got mad when press reports blamed her father for all of her troubles. While he had been an enormous influence on her life, Capriati didn't hate him. She still loved both of her parents.

At the end of her counseling program, Capriati and her parents moved from Florida to California. They all hoped it would be easier to get off to a fresh start in a new place.

That September, Capriati was in the news again. The Women's Tennis Association adopted the new age-eligibility rules that were proposed by the WTC. The object of the new rules was to prevent young players from burning out or being taken advantage of. No players under the age of fifteen would be permitted to compete on the tour, and until the age of eighteen they would be allowed to make only a limited number of appearances. The press referred to the regulations as "the Capriati Rules." Ironically, the first impact of the rules was to cause two fourteen-year-olds, Venus Williams and Martina Hingis, to turn pro before the rules went into effect.

Ever so slowly, Capriati was pondering a return to tennis. Despite the fact that she wasn't ranked anymore, tournament organizers kept sending her invitations to play. They knew their tournament would receive some free publicity if Capriati showed up on the court.

She finally accepted an invitation to play in Zurich, Switzerland, in October, but as she tried to work back into shape, she pulled a groin muscle and had to withdraw. A month later, the injury was healed, and she accepted an invitation to play in a tournament in Philadelphia. Her opponent in the first round would be Anke Huber, the number 13 player in the world.

No one quite knew what to expect when Capriati walked onto the court. She didn't keep them in suspense for long. From the first serve, it looked as if Capriati had never stopped playing. She was a little heavier than when she had last played, but she still demonstrated her patented style, blasting powerful forehands and double backhands from the baseline, spiced by the occasional charge to the net. Although she dropped the first set 4–6, she won the second 6–3.

Then she ran out of steam. Huber won the third set 6–1 to take the match.

Capriati bravely showed up at the postmatch press conference. "It felt good to be out there," she said, admitting, "I got tired. I'm not used to running like that."

Although tournament officials had asked that the questions be restricted to the match, the media couldn't resist asking about her recent troubles.

"I learned that it doesn't matter to me whether I win or lose," she said. "I just wanted to compete again. I experienced a lot. I got wiser. I think I found out what makes me happy. I learned about myself."

Although she said she hoped to play again soon, she withdrew from the doubles competition the next day with a sore shoulder, then pulled out of the

Australian Open with the flu. Throughout the rest of the 1995 season, everyone kept waiting for Capriati to play again. She never did.

Simply entering a few events didn't mean that she was ready to resume playing full time. Capriati wasn't in good enough physical condition to complete the season, and there were also other issues. Her parents' marriage was breaking up, and they would eventually divorce. Capriati knew that her troubles had been stressful for them, and she hated seeing them split up.

She also wasn't prepared to face the media day after day. Since her arrest, many reporters had blamed her mother and father for pushing her too hard, too soon. Despite everything she had gone through, Capriati still loved her parents and didn't blame them for her troubles. She hated answering the same questions over and over about her arrest and early career.

But beyond all that, Capriati was still emotionally fragile. Although she loved playing tennis, she didn't always like the way tennis made her feel about herself. Despite what she had told the reporters in Zurich, losing was hard for her to take, and physical injuries simply reminded her that she was out of shape. Tennis was no longer a joy — it was a job.

As far as she was concerned, until she could learn to be happy whether she won or lost on the court, there was no reason to keep playing.

Chapter Seven:
1996–98
Returning to Tennis

After Jennifer's parents divorced, her father moved back to Florida. Jennifer joined him and began preparing another return to tennis. Their relationship had changed. For years, he had been her coach first and her father second. But now, the decision to play tennis or not was hers alone. Once she decided to play again, she needed her father for both his emotional support and his input as a tennis coach. He knew her game better than anyone else did.

Jennifer didn't rush her return. She worked out and played a great deal of tennis to build her stamina. She knew that she couldn't just step onto the court and be a top-ten player again. After all, it had been nearly four years since she had been on the tour full time. When she'd pulled back from tennis, she was a seventeen-year-old kid. Now she was a young woman.

Slowly, she began to regain her love of the sport and was able to find perspective on winning and losing. She realized that the most she could do was work hard and play as well as she could. If she became a top-ten player again, great, but if she didn't, that was okay, as long as she was having fun and playing her best. As she explained when she made her return in February 1996, "I'm back because the one thing I've learned is that I love this game."

She started off slowly, usually winning one or two rounds early in a tournament and then falling to a more talented player in the middle rounds. While she didn't like losing, it was a little easier playing without being the center of attention. Earlier in her career, she had usually been the biggest story of almost every tournament she played, the young phenom whom everyone was watching. Now she was just another player on the tour.

In April, she reentered the WTA rankings as number 103. But Capriati had no illusions about her game. After losing in the first round of the French

Open, she withdrew from Wimbledon, feeling that she wasn't ready to compete at the Grand Slam level.

By the fall, however, her game had started to return. She was slowly rising in the rankings and was beginning to beat some top players. Entering a tournament in Chicago, Capriati was ranked number 50. Then she put together a great run of tennis, beating the number one player in the world, Monica Seles, in the semifinals to reach the finals of a tournament for the first time in more than three years. Although she lost in three sets to Jana Novotna in the final, her performance gave her some confidence and lifted her to number 24. At the end of the season, the WTA named her the Comeback Player of the Year.

But Capriati knew she still had a long, long way to go. An entire new generation of stars had arrived on the scene, and the women's tour was more competitive than it had been in years. The players who had been champions when Capriati first joined the tour, like Martina Navratilova, Gabriela Sabatini, and Steffi Graf, had either retired or were preparing to. The big stars were now players like Martina Hingis, Lindsay Davenport, and Venus Williams. Now Capriati was often older than her opponent. Many of them played the same style of tennis that Capriati had first brought to the tour so many years before, a powerful brand of the game that fans found exciting.

Over the next two years, her comeback stalled. Although she would occasionally play well in a tournament, she was inconsistent, as likely to lose in the first round to an unheralded player as she was to fight her way close to the finals. She was also hampered by a string of injuries. In 1997, a bad ankle sprain knocked her out of competition for more than three months, and she slipped all the way down to number 66 in the rankings. Then, in 1998, an elbow injury prevented her from playing until March. She never got back on track that year and dropped down to number 101.

When she began the 1999 season with a series of disappointing losses, most tennis observers were ready to write off her career. Although she'd tried hard, she had never quite gotten back to where she had once been. Perhaps, thought some, it was inevitable. When Capriati had been successful, she had been an adolescent, a strong five foot seven and 135 pounds. But during her time away from tennis, she had grown into adulthood, adding an inch and a half of height and several pounds to her frame. To some, it seemed as if her body had betrayed her, and she was no longer quick enough to be one of the top players in the world. That sometimes happened to athletes who had success when very young.

Yet even though her career appeared to be reaching an end, Capriati was still growing as a person. She finally felt as if she had come out of what she later described as "a very dark place." Although she didn't like losing, when she did lose she didn't act as if it were the end of the world. Now she knew that her friends and family cared for her whether she won or lost.

In a strange way, that knowledge may have been just what she needed. In the back of her head, she had worried that her worth as a person depended on how well she played tennis. Over the last two years, even though she hadn't played very well, she still felt good about herself. It was almost as if she had been testing herself by losing.

She had passed with flying colors. And now that she had learned that she didn't need to win, for the first time in a long time she really wanted to.

Chapter Eight:
1999

Comeback

In March of 1999, Capriati called former men's tennis star Harold Solomon, who was now a coach. She wanted Solomon to work with her.

Solomon was skeptical. He had seen her play over the past few years, and although he still believed she was a skilled player, he wasn't sure if she was committed to all the hard work it would take to get her back on top. He had heard through the tennis grapevine that after practicing diligently for a week or two, Capriati tended to lose interest.

But Capriati wouldn't take no for an answer. Over the course of a two-hour telephone conversation, she convinced Solomon that she was ready to make a total commitment to tennis again. Solomon agreed to become her coach.

"She convinced me," he recalled later. "I told my

wife, 'Maybe I'm crazy, but I believe her.' I could tell by the tone in her voice she really wanted it this time. It was now or never." Now that Capriati believed in herself, that's all she needed.

Solomon forced her to work hard. Capriati knew that if she didn't, he'd stop coaching her. If that happened, she realized everyone in tennis would get the impression she'd given up again. In April, she agreed to leave the tour to spend an intense month training and practicing. Solomon felt she needed to get in better physical shape.

Solomon didn't just help Capriati with her game or fitness. He helped her with her attitude. When she returned, he wanted the other players on the tour to be afraid of her.

"When a [Jimmy] Connors or [a Chris] Evert walked out there, the other player would feel them, their talent, their aura," he explained. "That's what they used to feel against Jennifer. We wanted them to know that Jen meant business." To that end, he made sure that when Capriati was practicing or working out, she did so where the other players could see her, and that she started early in the morning and ended late at night. He wanted every other player on tour to know that Capriati was back and working harder than anyone else.

When she returned to the tour in early May 1998 for a tournament in Berlin, Germany, she came back as a different person. Out of nowhere, she defeated four opponents, all in straight sets, to reach the finals, her first final since January of 1997. Then she crushed Elena Likhovtseva to win the tournament, her first victory in more than six years!

From Berlin, she went directly to the French Open. Since many of the top players had skipped the Berlin tournament to prepare for the French Open, few observers thought Capriati's victory meant very much. They thought she'd just gotten lucky against a weak field.

But now Capriati had some confidence, and she charged through her opponents. "I'm replenished, rejuvenated," she said after defeating Silvia Farina to reach the quarterfinals. "I know what people were saying about me. For a while I was afraid to go onto a tennis court again, to go out to see people. But I was always a fighter when I played, and I fought my way back to what I want to do. This. This is me. For the first time in a long time I'm having more fun on a tennis court than anywhere else." All of a sudden, the player everyone had forgotten about appeared to be back.

She faced number 2, Lindsay Davenport, in the quarterfinals. Although Capriati played well, Davenport defeated her in straight sets.

In the past, a loss in a Grand Slam event would have sent Capriati into a tailspin. But now she used the defeat as a measuring stick for what she still had to do. She got right back to work and set her sights on Wimbledon.

Once again, she played impressively. She drew number 30, Anke Huber, in the first round — a tough start for the tournament. After the two players split the first two sets, the third set ended in a 5–5 tie when the match was suspended because of darkness. When it resumed the next day, Capriati hung on for a 9–7 win. Although she lost in the second round, she was already looking ahead to her next challenge, the U.S. Open.

Eight years before, Capriati and Monica Seles had played one of the most memorable matches in tennis history when they had met at the Open as a couple of teenagers. This year, when they made it to the fourth round to face each other again, it was a great moment.

Seles had had problems, too. In 1993, when she was the number one player in the world, a mentally ill fan had stabbed her. Although she had recovered physically, she'd had a difficult time resuming her career. Just the fact that Seles and Capriati could play each other in an important match again was a victory for both of them.

For many tennis fans, the match was their first glimpse of Capriati in years. She looked great, and the crowd cheered loudly for both players, knowing that each of them had worked extremely hard to get to where they were. But Capriati was still a work in progress. Although she played well again, Seles won.

After the match, Capriati was expected to appear at a big press conference to discuss the match. Since her return, she'd grown tired of talking about her troubled past. She wanted to be recognized for what she was becoming, not what she had been.

At the beginning of the press conference, she read a short, prepared statement: "The path I took for a brief period of my life was not of reckless drug use, hurting others, but a path of quiet rebellion, of a little experimentation of a darker side of my confusion in a confusing world, lost in the midst of finding my identity." One writer called it "a sort of declaration of independence from her past and well-publicized troubles," while her brother, Steven, said, "It released the stress and anger inside. . . . My sister stood her ground and said 'Enough is enough.'"

Still, some members of the media asked her questions she didn't want to answer. Capriati broke down and started crying. "I just wish I didn't have to talk about this stuff all the time," she said before rushing off.

Some sportswriters thought her outburst was a sign that she wasn't ready for the pressures of tennis, but Capriati was looking ahead, not backward. Her performance lifted her all the way up to number 30, and she continued to play well for the rest of the year, winning another tournament in Quebec and reaching the semifinals in Philadelphia to finish the year ranked number 23.

She finally felt confident enough to talk a little about what she had gone through when she wasn't playing tennis. She knew that if she did, the press would finally stop asking her about it.

"I've stopped looking in the mirror and seeing a monster," she explained to one reporter. "I realized that my life doesn't have to be dark and ugly. I have a choice if I'm going to be happy or miserable, and I don't want to be on this earth living miserably.

"There were so many negative things said about me in the press," she added, "and they started outweighing the positives. I didn't like the way my face or body looked. I felt fat. I thought no one liked me because of this tennis thing, and I couldn't even do that . . . so I felt very lonely."

Things were different now, she explained. "I'm at peace with what's on the inside," she said. "I realize that there's life after tennis, and even though I don't know what it is yet, it's gonna be fun to find out when I'm done with the game. In the meantime, I'm just trying to do the best I can."

And the best she could do was suddenly very, very good.

Chapter Nine:
2000–01
Rising Up

Capriati's steady improvement continued in 2000. She opened the year by winning the Millennium Cup exhibition tournament in Hong Kong, defeating Martina Hingis, ranked number one, in the final. There was no question anymore. Jennifer Capriati was back and once again was one of the best tennis players in the world.

At the Australian Open, she served notice as to just how far she had come, reaching the semifinals. Her opponent was Lindsay Davenport. It was a tough match, but Capriati lost on a second-set tiebreaker. After the match, Harold Solomon told her, "Look, you're right there. We either work ten percent harder and ride this thing to the top or we slack off and go the other way. Which is it?"

Capriati told him she wanted to keep working.

But then she got sidetracked, at least for a little while. She started seeing a handsome Belgian tennis player named Xavier Malisse, whom her mother described as "her first real boyfriend." Happy with herself, Capriati decided that it was time to have some fun and enjoy life.

Unfortunately, that didn't leave quite so much time for tennis and working out as before. Although Capriati had a great time over the next six months or so, her progress under Solomon stalled even as she climbed to number 12 in the rankings. In April, she and Solomon decided to go their separate ways. Soon afterward, Capriati announced that her father was again coaching her.

The tennis world held its breath. Although those close to Jennifer acknowledged that Stefano Capriati knew his tennis, many wondered if it was a good idea for her to be coached by her father again.

But both the daughter and the father had grown up. Each had the relationship in perspective. As Stefano said later, "I know her game better than anyone, but she's a woman, not a girl now. My role is more as a dad than a coach."

Staying close to her family was becoming more

important to Jennifer Capriati. Her mother had moved back to Florida, then had been diagnosed with cancer and had to undergo hip surgery. Although Jennifer's parents were still friends and lived near each other, she felt that it was up to her to help her mother through her recovery.

When the 2000 season ended, Jennifer finally had the time to focus on training again. She broke up with her boyfriend and was determined to continue her comeback. Over the two-month break, she spent hours every day exercising and practicing. Working with a personal trainer, she got in the best shape of her life.

When she returned to the tour in 2001, people hardly recognized her. Capriati was ripped. Her arms bulged with muscles, and she exuded strength and confidence. And when she stepped onto the court at the Australian Open, she played that way.

Observers noted that in addition to her expected power, she now exhibited patience. In the fourth round, she trailed Marta Marrero 1–5 in the first set, but remained calm and rallied to win 7–5, 6–1. Then playing against Monica Seles, she was down a set before bouncing back to storm into the semifinals.

That wasn't a huge surprise. After all, Capriati was still ranked in the top twenty. But few observers expected her to go much further. She had never won a Grand Slam event before, not even when she had been at the top of her game, and many tennis observers believed she never would. She always seemed to choke in the big matches.

But this was a new Jennifer Capriati. She dumped number 2 Lindsay Davenport in the semifinals, setting up a finals matchup versus number one Martina Hingis. During a press conference before the match, Capriati was focused and serious. "I didn't get to this point just to get to this point," she said. In other words, she wanted to win.

The two athletes represented contrasting styles. Hingis played finesse tennis. Her game depended on the precise placement of her shots and her ability to scurry back and forth across the court to make returns. Capriati's game, on the other hand, was pure power. She just kept hitting the ball as hard as she could and tried to blast her opponent off the court.

Capriati won the first set 6–4 and the second set 6–3. It was clear that she was on her game and

Hingis was not. At match point, Capriati pounced on a forehand and rifled a rocket down the line past Hingis.

For a moment, time seemed to stop for Jennifer Capriati. Ever since she had been a young girl, she had dreamed of winning a Grand Slam tournament. But she'd slipped and struggled so much since then that it hardly seemed possible. But her dream had come true.

Capriati didn't know how to react. With a stunned look on her face, she jumped up and down a few times, shook Hingis's hand, then dropped her racket and raced over to where her father was sitting in the stands. They didn't say anything to each other but just hugged.

"Who would have thought I would have made it here after so much has happened?" she wondered afterward at a press conference. "Dreams do come true."

"It was an amazing feeling. I can't even describe it; the whole two weeks were just fantastic."

But she was already looking ahead, saying she couldn't wait to see "what this new confidence I have after winning this tournament will bring. Who knows what can happen?" Now that Capriati was on top again, she didn't want to go back down. Her win lifted her to number 7 in the rankings, her highest point since 1993.

Over the next few months, Capriati secured her position as one of the best tennis players in the world, reaching the semifinals or finals in every tournament she entered except one.

She even seemed to be enjoying herself, particularly when she spoke to the press. All the questions were about how she was playing now, rather than about the past. She still didn't see much sense in talking about that. "I don't get into that whole bad-girl-makes-good hype," she told a reporter. "I just hope people who are down or don't feel good about themselves can see this and use it as inspiration."

At the French Open, Capriati provided even more inspiration. She was one of the favorites to win the tournament.

She raced through the early rounds and faced Martina Hingis in the semifinals. Capriati got off to a quick start and was leading the first set 4–1 when she wrenched her knee. She had to pause to receive treatment.

When the match resumed, Hingis took advantage and quickly tied it at 4–4. But Capriati hung in to win the set. Then in the second set, as one writer described it, "she ground [Hingis] into powder."

"Right now," said Hingis after the match, "Jennifer Capriati is the best player in the world. She overwhelmed me."

Only Kim Clijsters stood between Capriati and her second consecutive win in a Grand Slam event. The two played a classic match.

Capriati lost the first set 1–6 and won the second 6–4. Then she and Clijsters dug in for an unforgettable finale.

Nearly every point resulted in a long rally as both players tried their best to beat the other, Clijsters putting her powerful forehand and retrieving ability against Capriati's potent backhand. Finally, on match point, Capriati whipped a forehand by her opponent to win the final set 12–10. She was the French Open champion!

This time she celebrated like a boxer, raising both hands above her head. "I never thought I'd be standing here eleven years later after playing my first time here when I was fourteen years old," she said after the match. "Really, I'm just waiting to wake up from this dream."

But for now, Capriati didn't mind dreaming just a little bit longer. She deserved it.

Chapter Ten:
2001–02
More to Do

As soon as she won the French Open, there was speculation that Capriati could actually win the Grand Slam, which would entail winning both Wimbledon and the U.S. Open. Kim Clijsters said, "I think she'll win one more Grand Slam [event] for sure."

Everything had started happening very quickly once Capriati started winning. Over the past year, she had signed some modest endorsement contracts. So just as she was playing great tennis again, it became harder for her to stay on top, because now there were more demands on her time.

This time around, however, Capriati knew how to deal with the obligations of fame. Exhausted the week before Wimbledon, she withdrew from a tournament to rest. But the break may not have been enough. At Wimbledon, she fought her way to the quarterfinals, where she defeated future champ Serena Williams. But then she seemed to run out of steam in the semifinals, losing to Justine Henin.

Although she was sad, she wasn't crushed. "When you lose, you always feel disappointment," she said. "But it helps that you lost to somebody [who] played well." When she was asked if she was upset that she had missed her chance at the Grand Slam, she just laughed.

"Not really," she said. "Everybody was making a big deal out of it but me. I'm pretty happy with the way the year has gone so far. It would have been nice, but, oh well."

There were other things far more important, like continuing to help her mother through her health crisis. Capriati also made sure that tennis remained fun this time around, telling people that the highlight of her year was playing with her brother, Steven, in the mixed doubles competition at Wimbledon. They lost, but she was thrilled that they were able to play together. As she said herself, "It's just part of my growing up, my maturity. . . . I've had a lot more losses, in different ways, than this tennis match."

Capriati continued playing well during the rest of

the year. Despite losing to Venus Williams in the semifinals of the U.S. Open, nothing could knock her off track. By the fall, she was ranked number one and had earned the respect of the tennis world. At the end of the season, she received all sorts of honors, such as being named the International Tennis Federation World Champion 2001 and the Associated Press Female Athlete of the Year. Then she began the 2002 season where she left off in 2001, by winning the Australian Open again, battling through 120-degree heat to defeat Martina Hingis in the final. Not only was Capriati back, she was back to stay.

"People were afraid that once I tasted success again I'd lose my motivation," she explained. She was determined not to let that happen. "I don't care about the stardom and the hype," she said. "The tennis is what matters to me. I look back on this year and I'm relieved, I'm happy. I guess it all makes for a good story, but it's not like it's over yet."

Jennifer Capriati has more she wants to accomplish. And the future is bright.